Always continue to dream!

Best,

Martin

W

hen is the best time to teach a child about life's values? The sooner the better! With the help of Sandy Cat, Dr. Martin Bednar transforms the true life story of Sandy Cat and Clarkie into a series of wonderful learning experiences for children (and adults!) of all ages.

Sandy Cat is an absolutely adorable stray tabby who appeared on our doorstep many years ago. Sandy's Vision is the true life story of a young boy, Clarkie, who develops a lasting bond with Sandy Cat, by helping Sandy recover from an illness that initially left him unable to walk or see. Clarkie learns to view life's obstacles and challenges as opportunities for learning, growth and achievement. Clarkie also learns to persevere, even when it's not very easy. In turn, he shares this valuable lesson with his cousins. Many years later, Sandy walks and sees and is just as adorable as ever!

In Sandy's Dream, Sandy Cat is the focus of a very interesting discussion: what do cats dream about? The children not only imagine the dreams that Sandy Cat may have, but also embark on a wonderful journey of what their own dreams could be. Their thoughts and dreams will both surprise and inspire you! In Sandy's Dream, Clark is now a young teenager, who has begun to think and see the world by how his actions impact others, a lesson that he again shares with his cousins.

Sandy was also the first animal in the world known to receive a combination therapy that may encourage the production new brain cells (neurons) that are lost after injury. One of these therapies is now being studied in people who have suffered a stroke!
And we all wonder ... was Sandy's 'chance' visit to our home that day really just a coincidence?

It was the perfect summer afternoon for Clark and his cousins
to visit Uncle Marty and Aunt Arlean in the country.
Fluffy, puffy clouds moved slowly and quietly across the blue sky above,
playing a game of hide and seek with the sun.

As soon as they arrived, the children scattered in all directions, trying to investigate everything at once.

They ran in the meadows, the tall grass tickling their arms and legs, as butterflies danced among the bright wildflowers.

They walked along the wooded paths while the birds chirped and sang, welcoming them to their home. And they knelt by the edge of the pond, hoping to see a rainbow turtle or to catch the giant bullfrog they were sure was hiding somewhere in the cattails.

Inside the house was Sandy Cat.
He had found his favorite spot.
His paws were carefully tucked under his soft, shiny coat.

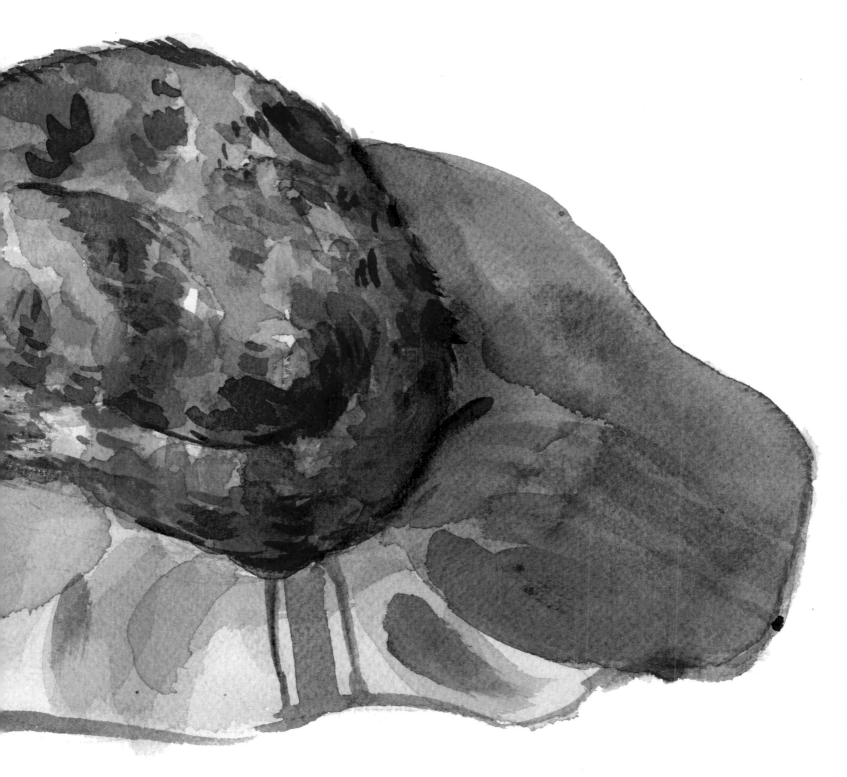

His tail stretched all the way around to nearly touch
his long, white whiskers.

The sunbeams were his blanket, and
his front paws were his pillow.

He was snoring very softly.
Sandy Cat was fast asleep

N ow in a race for the house, Clark, Timmy, Kylie, Jordan, Tori, Randy and Marty Jr. came in to see Sandy.

"Sandy was very sick for a long time, but now he is feeling fine," said Clark.

He spoke very quietly, so he wouldn't wake him.

"We went to the doctors together when Sandy couldn't eat, and I helped take care of him when he came home.

Sandy liked that a lot and we become good friends", he said with a big smile. "Sandy doesn't run and jump outside anymore, but he can walk everywhere in the house and he wants to know what is in every room. Sandy is a very curious cat!"

Tori whispered, "Aunt Arlean, do you think Sandy dreams when he is asleep?"

Before she could answer, Jordan said, "I think he does."

"Me, too," said Kylie and Timmy at the same time.

The other children nodded.

"Well," said Aunt Arlean, "what do you think Sandy dreams about?"

They all began to think.

Timmy spoke first, as usual.

"Mm fink-" His mouth was full of cake he loved to snack on, and no
    one could understand him.

He chewed very quickly for a moment and then gulped a big gulp.
All his cousins laughed.

"I think Sandy Cat dreams about eating cat treats,"

Timmy said. "I'll bet they're his favorite snack."

Tori was thinking of her two kitties at home as she looked at Sandy.

"My kitties love to play with the cats next door," she said.

"Sandy Cat probably misses the other kitties that he used to play with in the
meadow. I think that he dreams about running and playing with them.

While Tori talked, Randy had been hopping from one foot to the other and twisting his arms around each other.

He could hardly wait for her to finish.

The moment she stopped, he said quickly, "Guess what I think Sandy Cat dreams about-playing with his toys! I'm sure he loves to bat at the feathers and chase the bright little ball."

Randy stopped to think and then added, "I wonder if dreaming about playing with his toys makes Sandy Cat even sleepier."

Kylie was watching Sandy Cat very carefully,
She played with him a lot, and often wondered
what he might be thinking.

"Maybe he dreams about sleeping," she said. "Kitties love to nap, so maybe Sandy dreams of a nap in the warm sun- even while he is sleeping!"

All of her cousins and even Kylie looked a bit puzzled for a moment. As she thought more about this, she added with a big smile, "I wonder if he could do that. It would be so cool!"

Everyone nodded.

Jordan, always ready to play, was using his basketball as a seat.
He suddenly sprang up, the basketball now in his hands,
as if he were going to shoot it.

"Sandy can't run fast or jump anymore," he said.

"Maybe he is dreaming about being out in the meadow or in the woods,
running through the tall grass or climbing up a big tree or jumping to the very
top rock in the garden, where he could look over everything in the yard.
I bet he misses that."

Marty Jr. had listened to what his younger cousins were saying. They all had great ideas of what Sandy might be dreaming about.

Like them, he was thinking about Sandy.

But he also wondered what different people dream about when they sleep.

"Do you think that Sandy dreams like we do?" Marty Jr., asked.

Everyone looked puzzled.

Then Kylie asked, "What do you mean?"

Marty Jr., said "I wonder if Sandy dreams about other kinds of things besides the ones he enjoys, like eating and sleeping and running and playing."

No one answered. No one knew.

"Well," said Aunt Arlean, "maybe you can tell us what you dream about."

"Most of all, I dream of growing up and helping other people," he said.

Clark was listening carefully, remembering when Sandy was very sick and couldn't walk and couldn't see. In a soft voice he said,

"When I helped Sandy get better, I think he felt very special. And that made us both feel very, very good. So we should dream of making everyone around us feel very special, because this will make us all feel good."

Marty Jr. smiled and nodded in agreement.

"But how do you do that?" asked Tori.

"**W**henever you are kind to someone, at school or at home or when you're out playing with your friends, whenever you really listen to what someone else **is** saying, whenever you do something for someone else that you didn't have to do, you make them feel very special, and it makes you feel good too," said Clark.

"But if it's only in your dreams, then you really didn't do anything. What good is that?" Tori asked.

"You don't have to be asleep to dream, but you have to be awake to make those dreams come true," said Clark.

"So your dreams aren't done when you wake up?" asked Tori.

"No," said Clark. "They've just begun and that is when the fun begins, making your dreams become real, for you and for everyone around you.

Isn't that right, Uncle Marty?"

"Well," said Uncle Marty, "why don't we just ask Sandy?"

Sandy had just opened his eyes. He stretched a big, long stretch and yawned a big, wide yawn before he fluffed his soft sandy coat.

"**W**hat do you think, Sandy?", asked Clark.
With a swish of his tail, Sandy walked
over to Clark and gently rubbed
up against him.

Clark picked up Sandy and held him close.
"Purrrr-fect," Sandy purred with a loud
rumbling purr, as his paw reached up to touch
Clark's face.

And then Sandy snuggled in Clark's lap
to begin to dream another dream.

MEOW!

❦ DEDICATION ❧

Sandy's Dream was inspired by my nephew, Martin William Bednar Jr., who was named after his grandfather. At a very young age, Marty Jr. developed a special relationship with the grandfather he never met, having died just months before he was born. A school essay, below, that he wrote at age 7, provides the theme that his cousins and hopefully other children (and adults!) who read this book will learn and also share in their lives. In Sandy's Dream, readers of all ages are encouraged to live their dreams and to be inspired to live the most courageous and noble dream of all: achieving happiness and satisfaction in life through what they share with others.

This book is dedicated to my family, most especially to my father, Martin William Bednar, who taught me life's most important lesson of the equality of each and every person, through the example of his life. I will always miss him.

I have been blessed by a truly remarkable group of people who reinforce this powerful message and who inspire me by how they live their lives: my dear mother, Stella, my three siblings, Tom, Randy and Ginger, Bob Vlad and John Ruccolo, Dr. John C. McGiff, Fr. Raymond Suriani, Dr. Cordell Gross, John Flaherty and Alan Frohman.

And finally to my wife Arlean, who is my constant support and guidance in my pursuit of living this dream. Every day.

❦ MY GRANDPA ❧

I may never have met my grandfather, but I feel like I know him.

You see, when my mom was pregnant, my grandfather was battling cancer and died.

Even though he cannot be with me today, he continues to live in my heart.

My father tells me of the wonderful childhood he enjoyed because of my grandfather.

My grandfather was a policeman who liked helping others and made everyone around him feel special.

When I look at pictures of him, he is always smiling.

I love to hear stories about my grandfather.

When we visit New York, where I grew up, we always make a point of visiting

the cemetery to see him. I always tell him how I am doing and still talk to him like he is alive.

My name is Martin William Bednar II and I am proud to be named after him.